yogurt the ogre

The Colorful Tale of the Creative Crayon

Driven by optimism, fun, playfulness, and exploration, pdoink seeks to inspire families
to transform, perform, and grow. pdoink invents and realizes great stories that
enable learning and enjoyment for positive change and self-development.

The positively pdoinkian adventures of Yogurt the Ogre are timeless tales of self-reflection and
friendship led by a re-imagined ogre. We created these stories to help children learn
to care about people, the world around them, and themselves!

Because we are parents, we understand bedtime. The Colorful Tale of the Creative Crayon is a terrific 7 o'clock
story to share with your children. Read on, and you'll also find one of Yogurt's favorite tales at the end
of each book. While children love to read stories about Yogurt and his friends, Yogurt's favorite
poems are about children. These fun poems are designed to enhance the reading experience
for your children and, in a pinch, they make a great 8 o'clock story. Enjoy!

———————————

Yogurt the Ogre created by David Rendimonti
Bedtime Stories for Yogurt the Ogre created by Lawrence Hourihan
Yogurt the Ogre–The Colorful Tale of the Creative Crayon published by Shawna Sheldon
Writing by David Rendimonti, Lawrence Hourihan, Jessica Lowe, and Shawna Sheldon
Illustration by Agnes Garbowska
Book design by Gillian and Paul Sych

For our families—DR and LH

Please visit us at: www.pdoink.com

Copyright © 2011 pdo!nk Inc.

Published by pdo!nk Inc., Toronto, Ontario, Canada.

ISBN 978-0-9868013-2-7

This book was printed in Toronto, Canada, by C.J. Graphics Inc., www.cjgraphics.com,
using solar energy, wind power, and bio-derived inks, and on paper that has been certified
by the Forest Stewardship Council® and the Rainforest Alliance™.

10 9 8 7 6 5 4 3 2 1

yogurt the ogre

The Colorful Tale of the Creative Crayon

It was a spring day in Mudd Hollow and the air was wet and cool. Sunshine was poking her way through the clouds, and for a brief moment the leaves and flowers looked like sparkly treasures. But it was not long before a grumbling cloud rolled in and spoiled Sunshine's fun.

With a **hop** and a **skip** Yogurt the Ogre jumped out of his bed to discover an all too rainy day.

Yuck, thought Yogurt, as he gazed out his window at the gray sky. He watched fat drops of water bounce on the windowsill. "Pdoink, pdoink," they seemed to say. This was not a day for fun in the sun. But a little rain wasn't going to stop Yogurt, so off into the muck he trekked!

Yogurt was skipping to Copper Caterpillar's house when he spotted Copper just off the path munching on some leaves.

"Hi Copper! Do you want to play?"

Chomp Chomp Chomp

"I can't," he said between bites.

Chomp Chomp Chomp

"I'm sorry, Yogurt. I have to be home soon and I'm already late!"

Yogurt knew that when Copper had to go anywhere it took him a long time. Copper was easily distracted. Sometimes it was the pretty birds, other times it was the pretty flowers, but most times it was some pretty tasty leaves.

"That's okay, Copper. See you later." Yogurt waved goodbye to his friend and off he strolled.

Yogurt continued happily sloshing through the rain to Tumbleberry Bunny's house.

When Tumbleberry opened the door, Yogurt could see that she was very busy!

"Dad and I are baking a carrot cake for Mom's birthday!" shouted Tumbleberry over the banging and clanging from the kitchen. "Want to help?"

Yogurt watched as Tumbleberry's dad moved through the kitchen. He was working so fast that he was beginning to make Yogurt feel dizzy.

"Maybe another time!" Yogurt shouted as a great glob of batter flew over his head.

And Yogurt bounded into the rain once more.

Splash

Yogurt merrily made his way to Lady Blue Damselfly's house, skipping and kicking the puddles along the way. As he arrived at her front door, he heard her soft voice from up above him.

"Yogurt! Up here!" she shouted.

"I'm off to my grandma's for the weekend. See you next week," she said as she gave him a quick wave and flew away.

A disappointed Yogurt waved goodbye and slowly began his trip home.

When Yogurt arrived home he was very soggy, very tired, and a little grumpy. He stomped into the kitchen.

Clump Clomp Clump Clomp

"What's wrong, Yogurt?" asked Mom.

"All of my friends are busy and I can't play outside. There is NOTHING to do," he grumbled.

"Do you want to help me make lunch?" **"No,"** he said.

"Do you want to play a board game?" **"No,"** he said, once more.

"How about coloring? I picked up some new crayons for you."

Yogurt thought for a moment and then groaned, "Oooookaaay."

It sure was tough being Yogurt on a rainy day.

Yogurt laid out his new crayons on the floor in his room. He started drawing a big circle for Sunshine when... OOOPS! The crayon slipped off the paper. Yogurt frowned. He wanted to make Sunshine big and this paper just would not do.

Then his eyes turned to the big, smooth wall—it was perfect!

Yogurt teetered high on his toes and drew a HUGE Sunshine! This made his gloomy room feel brighter already! Yogurt started to forget about the rain altogether. He added birds and a bright rainbow using every color from the crayon box. Finally, Yogurt made a picture of himself with his friends—life-sized!

Then, from behind him he heard,

Oh my!

Yogurt turned to see Mom staring at the wall.
He smiled proudly. It DID look great.

But then Mom stared at Yogurt for a long, long, long, long time.

Yogurt knew that when Mom stared at him for a long, long,
long, long time, it was not a good thing...

...and Yogurt was right.

"You don't like it?" Yogurt asked in a tiny voice.

"I love your drawing, Yogurt," Mom replied. "But I am not
happy about where you put it. The walls aren't meant for
drawings, dear."

"But I worked really hard on it!" said Yogurt.

"I know, Yogurt. But drawings are meant for paper.
You are going to have to clean this up. Now, let's
go get some soap and water."

Yogurt began scrubbing.

Wish Wash
Wish
Wash

He scrubbed and he rubbed,
but the crayon would not come off! In fact,
it just smudged and made the wall look worse!
Yogurt soon gave up on his scrubbing and
made his way downstairs for dinner.

It is a well-known fact that ogres are hungry all of the time.
They love to eat and gobble and slurp and snack and
nibble and chomp and munch and chew.

But this night, Yogurt was not happy
and he barely touched his food.

"Yogurt, what's wrong?" asked Dad.

Yogurt told his dad about his day, about his picture, about
how hard he had worked to clean his wall, and how
he had just made a bigger mess.

"It will come on, Yogurt," his mom said with an encouraging smile. "You can try again tomorrow."

That night, Yogurt hopped into bed with a bedtime story, but he was not in the mood to read. He sat in the darkness of his room and stared at his wall. He could not fall asleep.

How will I get that wall clean? he thought to himself for a long, long, long time.

Eventually, Moonbeam's soft glow help soothe him to sleep.

The next morning Sunshine beamed brighter than ever.

But Yogurt woke up to his messy wall and remembered what he had to do. He got a bucket of soapy water and began scrubbing again.

He rubbed, **Swish Swish**

and he brushed, **Scritch Scritch**

and he buffed, **Squeak Squeak**

and he wiped,

SWOOSH SWOOSH

for the entire day!

Finally...

Ta dahhh!

The wall was clean again!

"Phew!" Yogurt sighed. "That was hard work!"

Yogurt was hungry from his scrubbing so
he made his way downstairs for a snack.
He chewed and he munched.
He guzzled and he crunched.

Yummmmy!

he said as he gobbled up every last bite.

Then he turned to Mom and Dad,
"I'm so glad I finally got my wall clean!
Now I know why crayons aren't meant for walls.
It's hard work to get the mess off!"

Mom and Dad smiled. Then Dad told Yogurt
that he had a surprise for him.

"Close your eyes and put out your hands."
This was Dad's favorite way to give surprises.

When he opened his eyes he was holding a giant pad of paper!

"Your mom told me how great your drawing was, and I was
hoping that you could make one for me to see," he said.
"You know, Yogurt, when you put your drawings on
paper, you can show them to me, and to Grandma,
and to Grandpa, and to all of your friends."

Yogurt wrapped Dad in a great big ogre hug.

"Thank you, Dad!" he said and he raced
off to his room.

Yogurt laid out his new paper and his crayons.
He started to draw another HUGE Sunshine.
This one looked even better than the first!
Then he made a rainbow. It was bigger and
brighter than his last! And birds too!

Finally, Yogurt drew a picture of himself and his
friends—Copper Caterpillar, Tumbleberry Bunny,
and Lady Blue Damselfly—and everyone was
playing together.

Yogurt was admiring his work, when he heard
his Dad's voice.

"OH MY!" Dad exclaimed.

Dad looked at Yogurt for a long, long, long, long time.
And when Dad looked at Yogurt for a long, long, long,
long time... Well, Yogurt didn't know what that meant!

Finally, Dad said, "These are the best drawings
I've ever seen, Yogurt!"

And Yogurt smiled so big it made his cheeks hurt.

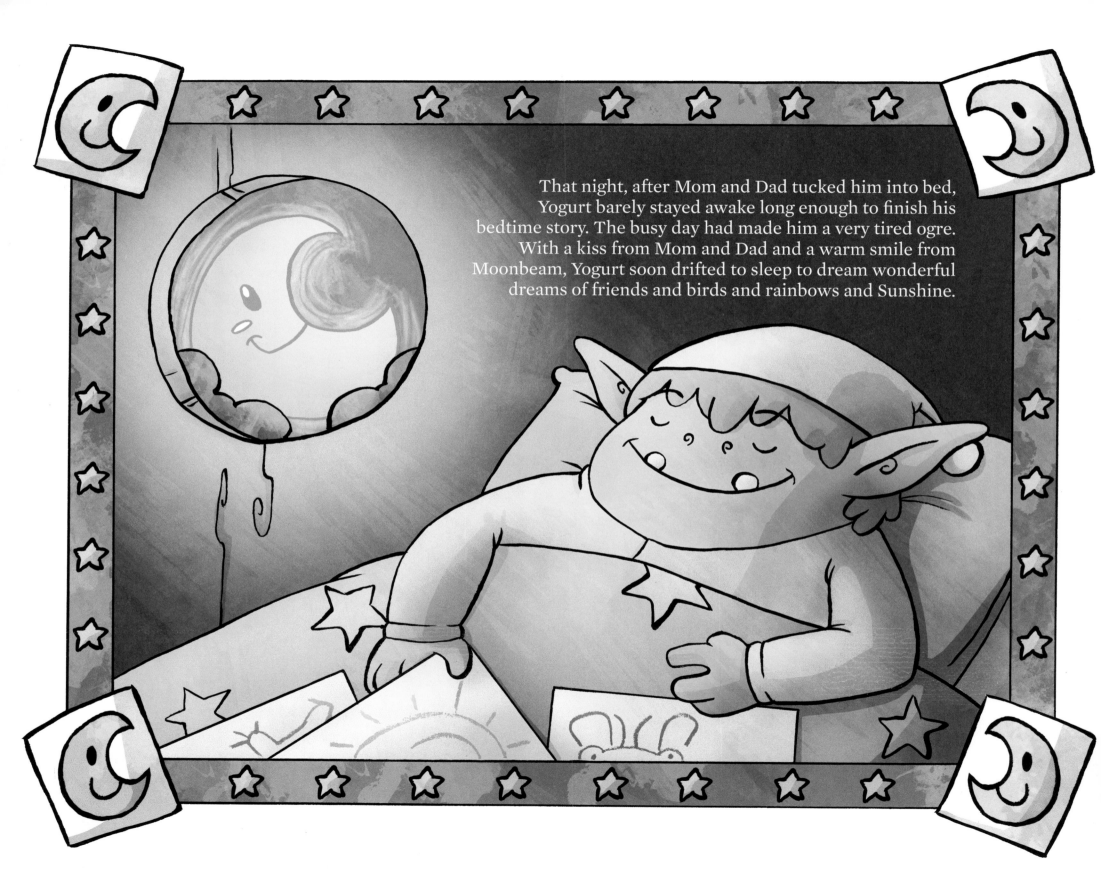

That night, after Mom and Dad tucked him into bed, Yogurt barely stayed awake long enough to finish his bedtime story. The busy day had made him a very tired ogre. With a kiss from Mom and Dad and a warm smile from Moonbeam, Yogurt soon drifted to sleep to dream wonderful dreams of friends and birds and rainbows and Sunshine.

TESS's MESS

A Bedtime Story for Yogurt the Ogre

With the sun brightly shining
And the sky painted blue,
Tess bounced out of bed,
Not sure what to do.

"I've got it!" cheered Tess
As she flew down the stairs.
"I'll be a clown.
I'll juggle apples and pears!"

But in the kitchen
The fruit had been taken.
So Tess grabbed an egg,
Some toast, and her bacon.

The toast soared up high
and the bacon went round!
But as for the egg,
Well it could not be found!

Then CRACK went the egg
As it plopped on the floor,
Wiggling and jiggling
As Tess ran out the door.

Next Tess was a pirate—
So brave and so mean.
But in her sword fight
She caused quite a scene.

She tripped on the sprinkler.
It sprayed to and fro.
She watched as it sprayed
Their clean windows, OH NO!

So soggy and wet,
Tess dashed away unseen.
Leaving large puddles
for Mom and Dad to clean.

Tess ran in the house
To find her sister, Heidi,
Who was painting a picture
And trying to be tidy.

Tess began dancing.
She started to kick!
She spun round and round
'Til she felt rather sick!

Then Tess took a stumble.
She knocked over the paint,
Coating poor Heidi,
Who cried in complaint:

"MOMMY! Please hurry!
Come look at this mess!
There's paint everywhere,
and it's all 'cause of TESS!"

Mom saw the puddles,
The egg, and the paint.
Mom saw the mayhem,
And she nearly did faint!

"A home's not a home
If you do not take care.
Please clean up your mess
And know what goes where!"

Tess washed up the messes,
Then went back upstairs.
She stacked all her books
And lined all her bears.

She placed her last toy
And she beamed full of pride
"A place for everything!
I did it!" she cried.

But soon as she finished
Their dog Flash was there.
He ran to her toys
Without any care.

With great loud
KERPLUNKS
Like rain the toys dropped!
All over the floor—
They could not be stopped!

Tess's lip trembled
As she watched her toys crash.
But she thought of Mom's words
And whispered to Flash:

"A home's not a home
If you do not take care.
But don't worry, Flash.
I'll show you what goes where."